*Deeply Regretted By …*

to Gordon Snell

Maeve Binchy

# Deeply Regretted By …

ARLEN
HOUSE

'Death in Kilburn', *The Irish Times*, 1978.
The publishers are indebted to The Irish Times Ltd for 'Death in Kilburn'.

First published by Turoe Press, an imprint of Arlen House, in 1979 in
association with the Drama Department, Radio Telefis Eireann.

Published in 2005 by Arlen House

PO Box 222
Galway
Ireland

Phone/fax 086 8207617
email: arlenhouse@ireland.com

ISBN    1–903631–50–5, paperback
        1–903631–70–X, hardback
        1–903631–90–4, limited edition

Typesetting: Arlen House
Printed by: Betaprint, Dublin

# CONTENTS

## PLAY PERFORMING RIGHTS

Application for the performing rights to this play must be made to

Christine Green, Authors' Agent,
6 Whitehorse Mews,
Westminster Bridge Road,
London SE1 7QD,
United Kingdom

who, upon payment of a fee, will issue a licence for the performance to be given. No performance may be given unless this licence has first been obtained.

# INTRODUCTION

## Louis Lentin

I have long been convinced that the most effective
television plays are of the slice-of-life variety and
whilst the subject, style and mood can vary
enormously, the best plays, whether recorded on
video tape or on film, are contemporary, and use the
intimate form of the television medium to deal with
extremely human situations.

Entertaining and socially relevant is a phrase I use
to express my preference for the type of play I would
like to see on RTÉ's Thursday Playdate. That is not to
say that I believe that all television plays should be
socially relevant, or if they are, that they must convey
a hidden message. Messages are for telegrams – not
for plays – and the short television play has nothing to
waste. The television play for me, whether it be
comedy or drama is at its most effective when you, the
viewer, looking at your small 21-inch screen in the
privacy of your own home can recognise in the
characters something perhaps of the guy next door
and can say 'I know someone that happened to ...' or
perhaps 'gee that's what happened to me'.

Of course many stage plays have been presented
well on television, but I find these are usually of a type
where the characters are powerfully dominant and the
setting passively simple. Television is the wrong
medium for the leisurely evocation of atmosphere. It is
also wrong for whimsy, fantasy and artifice. It is
absolutely right for realism. It is the extreme
performing medium for subtlety – at its best you can

perceive the thought behind the moment; the texture of life under a magnifying glass. It can be used to present a story and situation in strong simple terms to a large audience. It is a medium where word and image can and should complement, but where the image must be easily recognisable. It owes little to the feature film and less to the theatre. Used well it can provide the extra dimension to the facts of current affairs programmes. It takes over where they leave off, and is certainly more memorable.

Plays are about people, not about ideas; and it is a personal ambition that Thursday Playdate will achieve for Irish audiences what ABC Armchair Theatre achieved in England during the late fifties and sixties; where its simplicity, directness, social awareness and appeal complemented a new wave of writers in the theatre achieving a cross fertilisation that benefited both media.

One of the objects in publishing scripts from Thursday Playdate is not only to provide a closer contact with the well-written television play – but also to make these plays available for stage production. There is a dearth of good short plays for the theatre and particularly for the imaginative amateur director – the three plays published in this series are ideal. If he is prepared to examine them carefully I believe he will find that each will adapt to a fluid free production, that owes nothing to walls, flats and sets – but everything to character, situation and simplicity.

Shortly after reading 'Death in Kilburn' by Maeve Binchy in *The Irish Times* I asked her to write a television play based on the true story as told in that article. The result was the highly successful play *Deeply Regretted By ...*, Maeve Binchy's first play for television. *Deeply Regretted By ...* has won awards for the author in Ireland (Jacobs Awards) and at the 1979 Prague Television Festival (best script). It will represent RTÉ at the Prix Italia and has been invited to the prestigious first New York Television Festival later this year. Just how the structure of the play compares to the article you can see in this volume which contains both.

Shown twice already by RTÉ, it has affected audiences deeply and in a manner rarely achieved. It has done this because it tells its shocking, but extremely compassionately human story in a direct and simple manner, and in a way that is incredibly real. It doesn't point the finger, it doesn't blame. Nobody has got the answer. This is how life can be. Apart from presenting the story well Maeve Binchy has also given us characters that are completely alive, believable and eminently rewarding to perform. She has observed them well and has given them in her writing some wonderfully telling moments.

The play stems from the discovery of the late Mike Healy's two marriages, but goes on to say much about the meaning of people's lives. Audiences everywhere have reacted to Sean Healy's line:

Nobody at home thinks Mike lived in Kilburn. They think he worked in Kilburn, but he lived back home. That's where his place is, and his family.

The RTÉ drama department is to transmit Maeve Binchy's second play for television *Ireland of the Welcomes* in March 1980.

September 1979

*Deeply Regretted By ...* was originally broadcast on RTÉ in a Thursday Playdate series in 1979 with the following cast.

THE PLAYDATE CAST

| | |
|---|---|
| STELLA: | Joan O'Hara |
| FR. BARRY: | Donall Farmer |
| MARLENE: | Patricia Martin |
| JACKY: | Brian DeSalvo |
| SEAN HEALY: | Pat Layde |
| LIAM HEALY: | Eamonn Draper |
| DOCTOR: | Mona Baptiste |
| MRS. WYLEY: | Virginia Cole |
| CHILDREN: | Judy Beech |
| | Caoilfin Turner |
| | Rathnait Turner |
| | |
| Design: | Pat Molloy |
| Directed by: | Louis Lentin |

Patrick went into hospital on December 1st. He was sure he would be well home for Christmas, because it was only a light form of pneumonia, they told him. Modern drugs cured that kind of thing easily.

They didn't cure Patrick. He died on Wednesday, 7th, without very much pain.

Stella was negotiating about the Christmas turkey when the news came from the hospital. She couldn't believe it, she kept thinking that it was a huge hospital and they must have made a mistake.

She asked the priest to come with her to the hospital. He was a nice new priest who had come to the area a couple of years before, he wasn't attached to the parish church, he worked in welfare.

Father O'Brien went to the hospital with Stella and he asked all the right questions. It was a viral pneumonia, it hadn't responded to antibiotics. Nothing could have been done, his coming into hospital had just meant that he died with less discomfort and he had aids to his breathing up to the very end.

They were very sorry and they gave Father O'Brien and Stella cups of coffee out of a machine without asking them to pay for them. They told them to sit there as long as they liked.

Stella said they had better send telegrams to his mother and his brother in the West of Ireland, and Father O'Brien brought her back to his office to do this. They gave his office number as somewhere to ring, because Stella and Patrick didn't have a phone.

She went home by herself to tell the children when they got back from school. They had four children, and they all came home around 4pm. She bought a cake for tea because she thought it would cheer them up, and then she decided that it was too festive, the children would think they were celebrating or something, so she brought it back to the shop and they gave her the 65p back.

On Thursday, December 8th, the feast of the Immaculate Conception, the children were off school anyway. They sat around in the house while a neighbour made cups of tea for Stella and told her that she should thank her maker every hour of the day that Patrick hadn't been on 'The Lump' like so many of the men, and that there would be something to feed his wife and children with now that he was gone.

Stella agreed mechanically, felt a sense of cold all through her stomach. She still thought that Father O'Brien might run in the door with his face all smiles saying it had been a mistake, that it was another Patrick who had died of this thing that drugs couldn't cure.

But Father O'Brien was having a very different kind of conversation. Two men had arrived in the little office. They were Patrick's brothers, they had got the night boat over and come up on the train to Euston. It was their first time in London.

They hoped Father O'Brien would understand why they had come and appreciate the urgency of what they were doing. They were bringing Patrick's body back with them to the West. They had been given the name of an Irish undertaker who arranged funerals across the channel and they were going to see him now.

'But he's lived all his life here', said Father O'Brien. 'Won't he want to be buried here where his wife and children can visit his grave?'

'No', said the older brother, 'He'd want to be buried in the parish church at home, where his wife and seven children can visit the grave'.

Oh dear God, thought Father O'Brien to himself. Here we go. 'Well I think you'll have to discuss this with Stella', he began.

'We don't know anything about Stella', said the brothers.

'I'll take you to Stella's house', said Father O'Brien firmly.

The brothers agreed reluctantly that if it would avoid trouble they supposed they'd better go. Father O'Brien got someone to look after his telephone and they walked off past the shops that were all lit up with Christmas lights and plastic holly sprigs. Father O'Brien got rid of the children and the neighbours and sat through the worst conversation of his 15 years as a priest.

Somehow anything he had to take before was easier than watching a woman realise she had been deceived for years, seeing the peeling back of layer after layer, realising that on five occasions when Patrick had gone home alone to see his old mother he had managed to conceive another child.

He could barely look at Stella's face when the halting inarticulate sentences came out of the brothers, each one filling in a dossier of deceit and weakness and double dealing.

'What's she like ... your sister-in-law?' Stella said eventually.

'Like? Well she's a grand girl, Maureen, I mean she's had a hard life what with Patrick having to work over here and all, and not being able to get home except the once every summer'.

'But we were married in a church', said poor Stella, 'We must be really married, mustn't we Father?'

There was a throat clearing silence and Father O'Brien started to talk about God understanding, and Stella being truly married in the sight of God, and nobody being able to make hard and fast judgements about anything, and his voice petered out a bit.

The brothers were even more restless than Father O'Brien. With some kind of instinct that he still doesn't know how he discovered, he suggested that he take them for a pint because the pubs had just opened, and that he could come back and talk to Stella later.

He settled them in the corner and listened.

The story was simple. Patrick's funeral had to be at home, otherwise it was not a funeral. Otherwise his whole life cycle would have no meaning. It would be like being lost at sea not to be brought home to rest.

And that Englishwoman couldn't possibly come home with him and behave as a wife. They had nothing against the poor creature, it was obvious there had been some misunderstanding but Father could see, couldn't he, how much scandal there would be if she came the whole way over in black and brought her children with her, it would be flying in the eyes of God.

Father O'Brien's pint tasted awful.

And then there was the mother to think of, she had worked her fingers to the bone for the family, she was 83 now, they couldn't have a common law Englishwoman turning up at the Mass, now surely that was reasonable enough, wasn't it?

Stella was sitting where he had left her. She couldn't have moved from the table, and the door was on the latch the way he had left.

'Maybe there's a case for what they want to do?' he began.

'Sure', said Stella.

'It has nothing to do with the rules or laws or what the neighbours think, maybe there's just a case for letting him go back there to rest. It will give a lot of other people a lot of peace ...'

'Oh yes that's true', said Stella.

'And we can have a proper Mass for him here, too, you know', said Father O'Brien desperately.

'That would be lovely', said Stella.

'I've got to go back and tell them if you agree', he said glumly.

'What do you think is best?' she asked sadly.

'Well, I don't think anything is best, it all looks terrible and bitter, and I feel hopeless, but if you ask me what I want, I, I want Patrick to be buried here with you and his family all there to say goodbye.

'If you ask me what would bring the greatest happiness to the greater number then I think that you should let him be buried in Ireland'.

'It's a bit hypocritical, isn't it Father? Up to this morning you regarded us as a good Catholic family, part of your flock. Now suddenly I am an outsider, a woman living in sin, someone who can't go to a funeral in Holy Catholic Ireland in case I give scandal.

'I suppose the children are bastards as well. Everything that went before is all written off'.

'There's nobody who could say one word against you, Stella', he began.

'Except that my husband was really my fancy man, and I can't go to his funeral, myself and the four love children stay here while the wailing and the drinking and the praising and the caterwauling goes on in the West of Ireland, isn't that right?'

'It's not like that'.

'It is like that. And someone would say what a great man he was and how hard it is that emigration causes the break-up of families for so many people ... I'm not English, Father, I was born here but my parents were Irish, and know about funerals. I've heard them talk about them'.

'No one said life was fair', he said. 'It's been very cruel to you this Christmas'.

'Tell them they can have him', she said. She didn't come to the door, she wanted no Mass in Kilburn.

The brothers arranged with the undertaker and the body was taken to London airport and flown to Shannon and driven up the west coast and two weeks before Christmas on a cold Sunday afternoon Patrick was buried in a churchyard a mile from the house where he was born.

# Deeply Regretted By …

# LIST OF CHARACTERS

| | |
|---|---|
| FATHER BARRY: | Social worker priest – Irish |
| STELLA HEALY: | (Early 40s) – Born in Ireland. Has lived most of her life in England |
| SHARON:<br>MAUREEN:<br>GERALDINE: | aged 11<br>aged 6 – Stella's children<br>aged 8 |
| MARLENE: | Stella's neighbour |
| JACKY: | Young assistant to FR. BARRY in centre |
| SEAN HEALY: | (early 50s) Eldest brother of MIKE HEALY |
| LIAM HEALY: | (late 20s) Youngest brother of MIKE HEALY |
| MRS. WYLEY: | A client in centre |
| MR. COLLINS: | Client at the centre |
| DOCTOR | |

# SCENES

The play is set in Kilburn.

## PART ONE

## Scene One

*Shabby office – the welfare centre – it is not a presbytery, it's a working place where things get done. On the stairs leading to it there are posters and signposts.*

*FATHER BARRY is young, eager, and when we first meet him, totally in control of his work ... which involves a lot of fighting with institutions on behalf of individuals. He doesn't have any of the conventional stances of an Irish priest, he has no ceremony, no self importance, nor does he think he is always right. His faults, if he has any, are all centred around a boyish exuberant optimism. He could have his feet on the table.*

FR. BARRY: *(on the phone)* Yeah. Yeah. And what did you do then? Yeah. And what did he do then? Yeah. Well get to the terrible bit. *(pause)* That IS the terrible bit? Aw come on out of that, you're ringing me up and wasting my time telling me that one of your employees likes punk rock. Some of them might like Viennese Waltzes too, God forbid, and nobody's being phoned about it. Listen I don't want to hear from you again, no I mean it, I don't want to hear your voice on the phone unless you've a real complaint. Yeah Yeah Goodbye. *(he hangs up with a bang)* Bloody do gooder, bloody fat self-important Christian. That's what he is.

JACKY: I see what you mean about not apologising.

FR. BARRY: You're finished if you apologise, you'd never get any of them a job if you sounded a bit apprehensive on their behalf. Oh God I can't take employers like that. I really can't.

## Scene Two

*STELLA'S flat. It's a medium sized room, which has enough space for a table with four chairs around it, also two easy chairs. It's obviously the living room as well. It's in a council flat, remembering that council flats in Britain are less spartan than in Dublin. The furnishings are cheap. STELLA is saying goodbye to the children, fairly casually. The children are going into MARLENE'S.*

STELLA: Put those things away. I've got to go now. Come on Sharon.

SHARON: Can I bring teddy?

STELLA: Yes, alright. But not one word between you, I'll ask Marlene when I get back. Not a word of argument. Sharon chooses what channel and no fights. I want to be able to tell your Dad that you are being good.

GERALDINE: Can I come with you, Mam?

STELLA: No, I've told you before love, they don't like children in hospitals. Anyway, your Dad will be home in a day or two, so there's no point in annoying them.

*She brings the children to the door of MARLENE's flat and rings the bell. We can hear the TV or pop music from inside MARLENE'S flat.*

MAUREEN: Will he be home for Christmas?

STELLA: Of course he will, I'm just going to ask Matron exactly when.

MARLENE *opens the door.*

Marlene, thanks very much for taking them in again, and don't stand for a word of nonsense from them.

MARLENE: *(affectionately)* They're very good, they really are.

STELLA: They're not the worst, but thanks all the same, I'll be back in no time. Goodbye now – be good children, I won't be too long Marlene.

*She goes down the stairs.*

MARLENE: *(calling after her)* Take your time love. Don't forget the Irish paper this time.

STELLA: I won't. Bye.

MARLENE: *(ushering kids into her house)* In you go girls – who's for telly?

## Scene Three

*Interior large busy hospital. In a clerical office. An* INTERN *is going through a card index on the table. She finds the one she is looking for and turns back to the phone. Christmas music is heard from the tannoy system.*

INTERN: Right, yes I have it here. Mrs. Michael Healy. First name Stella, yes, I have it under next-of-kin. No phone, naturally. Yeah, Yeah. Will I get the messenger? Yeah. Well, she could be coming in now, it's five minutes to visiting time. Yeah. OK, no I'm not in a hurry. I'll do it. What did he die of anyway? Oh. I didn't know people died of that nowadays. Bye. Yes, I can handle it. It isn't the first time and I guess it won't be the last. Bye.

*She puts the phone down.*

## Scene Four

*Int. Hospital reception area. Visiting Hour. STELLA has just bought some flowers. She proceeds with other visitors along the corridor – the INTERN approaches her.*

INTERN: Mrs. Healy, Mrs. Michael Healy?

STELLA: Yes?

INTERN: I wonder could you come in here for a moment.

STELLA: Why – is there anything wrong?

INTERN: Please, I'd appreciate it if you'd just come with me *(she leads her to an adjacent room).*

STELLA: What …

INTERN: I won't keep you a moment.

*She brings STELLA into a small office and closes the door. She sits STELLA down and brings her a glass of water.*

INTERN: I've bad news for you. It's about your husband.

STELLA: What about my husband?

INTERN: I'm afraid he died this morning. I'm very sorry.

*STELLA shocked and with marks of tears on her face.*

STELLA: But nobody dies of pneumonia, they don't die of it. Could it be a mistake?

INTERN: *(gently)* I'm afraid there's no chance of a mistake Mrs. Healy.

STELLA: But pneumonia isn't a thing people die of. Not any more.

INTERN: It was a special kind of pneumonia, a viral pneumonia ...

STELLA: But what were the tests for and the drugs, and the bits of 'he's doing fine Mrs. Healy' what was all that for? *(head in hand, a look of total confusion on her face)* He can't be dead.

INTERN: Look – can I ring someone for you, Mrs Healy, is there a relative maybe, or friend, or a neighbour.

STELLA: Maybe Father Barry would be able to help me a bit.

INTERN: *(getting out a black address and phone number book)* Father Barry. Down at the presbytery?

STELLA: *(dully)* No, he's in a sort of centre, *(her voice trails away)* a kind of advice place.

INTERN: Oh, I know the place you mean, St Anthony's in Quex Road.

STELLA: Yes. I think that's it.

INTERN: I'll give him a ring for you right now.

STELLA: If he's not too busy.

INTERN: You just stay right here and leave everything to me – I won't be a moment.

*She leaves STELLA alone.*

## Scene Five

*Centre.* FR. BARRY'S *office. The phone rings.* JACKY *picks up phone.* FR. BARRY *is dealing with client – silent client's name –* MR. COLLINS.

FR. BARRY: Of course we haven't tried everything, there's a lot of things we haven't tried yet, we haven't got on to the Citizen's Advice Bureau, we haven't tried getting any publicity, we could ring the local paper, they'd love a story like this, they'd lap it up.

JACKY *interrupts.*

JACKY: Excuse me Father, it's the hospital, they've a woman there whose husband died of pneumonia. Healy they said the name was.

FR. BARRY: *(puzzled)* Healy. Healy? Not old – what's his name Healy, no, there's nothing wrong with him. Here, give it to me anyway. *(into the phone)* Hallo, Jim Barry at the centre here, can I help you? Yes, that's right, yes I do indeed. Oh dear God, that's very bad news indeed. That's very sudden. What happened to him? Yes, Yeah. Yes. I know. I know. No, of course I'll come over. Right, St. Martin's Ward. Right. Yes, yes. I know. Tell her I'm on my way. No, I'll find you don't worry. Goodbye.

JACKY: Bad news?

FR. BARRY: Mike Healy, a young man, with a wife and three children, went into hospital with a bad chest, and he died this morning. I'd better get down there fast.

JACKY: Do you think you'll be long?

FR. BARRY: I don't know, if Stella, the wife has someone down there, I might only be an hour. It depends.

JACKY: What about Mr. Collins?

FR. BARRY: *(turning around and laughing at him in a sending up sort of way)* What about Mr. Collins? You'll attend to Mr. Collins, Jacky boy, you'll do all the things that you want to do when you see me doing them, and you'll do them right, and by the book. I couldn't leave you in better hands, old stock. Right, I'm off –

*He goes.* JACKY *sits at* FR. BARRY'S *desk.*

JACKY: Right, Mr. Collins, I'm afraid we're going to have to start again from the beginning – you can't stay where you are because your sister is being re-housed and you have to leave the flat you're in, but there's no room for you in your sister's flat – is that it?

## Scene Six

*Interior hospital. FR. BARRY enters busy reception area. Asks for STELLA at desk. Strides down corridor with an air of authority.*

*Hospital reception area. STELLA sits alone. FR. BARRY comes striding down the corridor to where STELLA is. He grips her hand with both of his and he is very sincere in his sympathy.*

FR. BARRY: Stella you poor thing, this is terrible news, terrible, the poor man. Have you been here long?

STELLA: Not long at all Father, I came to visit him normally you know, I was just coming at visiting time *(her voice breaks)* and they were just about to send out to tell me.

*She cries.*

FR. BARRY: Go on cry away, don't be choking it back.

STELLA: It's not fair, he wasn't really sick at all.

FR. BARRY: I know I know, but you've got to believe he's better off where he is, not fighting for breath in a bed there with machines. He's at peace. You're the one that needs a bit of attention now. Where are the children?

STELLA: They're in my neighbour's house, in Marlene's, she's keeping an eye on them.

FR. BARRY: Good, they can stay there for a bit.

STELLA: I'll have to send his mother a telegram, Father, or maybe it'd be better for me to try and telephone one of his brothers, not to have the old woman getting a telegram. I was going to go to the Post Office.

FR. BARRY: You can't be going to a Post Office the week before Christmas, there'll be four thousand people in the queues. Come back to my office and send your telegrams and make your phone calls from there. Now let's get out of this place.

STELLA: Do we have much to do about Mike?

FR. BARRY: *(they rise)* Would you like to see him Stella – Mike?

STELLA: No – I don't think so Father. I'd prefer to remember him as he was.

FR. BARRY: Right then, Let's find Sister. After that, we'll take you back to my office. I'll arrange the Mass and everything.

*They go down the corridor.*

## Scene Seven

FR. BARRY'S *office later.* FR. BARRY *enters with* STELLA. *She is still carrying the paper and the flowers she had bought for* MIKE.

FR. BARRY: Sit down Stella.

JACKY: Oh, there you are Father. I didn't know if you were ever going to come back. Could you ring Mr. Petrie immediately. He says he's having problems with that boy we sent him yesterday. He wouldn't tell me about it – it was only for your ears.

FR. BARRY: Yes Jacky, in a minute. Sit down there Stella. Jacky, this is Mrs. Healy. I'd like you to get her a nice cup of tea. We have to send a telegram to Ireland and make a few calls.

JACKY: Oh, I see, I am sorry, of course. Right away.

STELLA: I don't want to be any trouble.

FR. BARRY: You're no trouble, you're in the right place. Now, let's think. *(he pulls a pad towards him)* Mike's mother is probably getting on a bit; you think it would be better to deal with one of the brothers?

STELLA: Well in a way it would be better, wouldn't it? I mean he could let the mother know then couldn't he?

FR. BARRY: So what's the eldest brother's name. I suppose he's the one we should reach.

STELLA: There's Sean and there's Martin and there's Liam, do you know I don't know which of them's the eldest.

FR. BARRY: Which of them *looks* the eldest?

STELLA: Well I never met any of them so I wouldn't know. But I think he used to talk about Sean more. *(she notices that* FR. BARRY *is surprised)* Well you know he just went home to please the old mother every year, he never stayed long, it would have been a terrible expense bringing myself and the girls, and sure our life is here and his was too, not there.

FR. BARRY: *(reassuringly)* Oh I know, I know.

STELLA: I think Sean has a phone.

FR. BARRY: Where's this he told me he came from?

STELLA: Ahaderg – Father.

FR. BARRY: Ahaderg, that's the place – somewhere in Co. Mayo I think. It might be in the Irish phone book, hold on a minute. Jacky would you throw me the Irish telephone directory, no that's the Dublin bit, the other one. Right. Now Sean Healy. Sean Healy.

STELLA: Or did Mike say that the phone was under someone else's name?

FR. BARRY: Well there's no Sean Healy listed for Ahaderg. Never mind we'll send a telegram, and give this number here if they want to ring us back.

STELLA: Ring us back?

FR. BARRY: Well to know the funeral arrangements and everything. We should leave them as much time as possible. They've a long way to travel.

STELLA: They mightn't want to come over at all.

FR. BARRY: Oh they'll come, they wouldn't mind if it was America, we may have to delay it a day for them, but they'll come.

STELLA: What will you say? *(she watches him writing)*.

FR. BARRY: Suppose I say 'Deeply regret tell you Mike died peacefully, today. Please telephone Father Barry and I'll give my number. Signed Stella'. Would that do? Or should we say more?

STELLA: Oh I think that's plenty. There's no point in putting that he died of pneumonia because they'd never be able to believe it anymore than I do.

FR. BARRY: *(Looking at his draft telegram)* I might put 'Deeply regret tell you all' that's covering the bit about telling Mike's mother.

STELLA: That would be fine.

FR. BARRY: And their address, just the name of the townland I suppose that's enough?

STELLA: That's all Mike ever put on the money he sent his mother every week, he said everyone knows everyone there.

FR. BARRY: You might go over sometime yourself, when the brothers come over for the funeral they could strike up a friendship, and you could take the girls to their Daddy's place sometime. You'd never know.

STELLA: *(doubtfully)* It might happen.

FR. BARRY: *(briskly)* Here's the tea, good man Jacky. Stella is there anyone else you want to ring, while you have a phone, any of your own relations or friends?

STELLA: They haven't got phones.

FR. BARRY: Any messages at all?

STELLA: *(bleakly)* No, I'll tell Marlene when I get back and she'll tell the neighbours for me.

FR. BARRY: Well we'll put a notice in the paper, the local one comes out on Friday so that's handy. I'll phone them tonight. Mike's body will be in the funeral home, we'll have the Mass on Friday. The undertakers will organise the grave and everything.

STELLA: You're very good Father.

FR. BARRY: The moment I hear from Sean or whoever, I'll tell them the details. Right, now, when you've finished that tea I'll take you home and then I'll have to run back here or Jacky'll have a heart attack.

STELLA: No honestly Father, I'd prefer to walk. I'd rather be on my own.

FR. BARRY: Are you sure?

STELLA: Yes, I'm sure Father.

FR. BARRY: Very well so –

STELLA: Goodbye Father, Goodbye ... er *(to JACKY)* Thank you very much, you're a real friend.

FR. BARRY: I did nothing. I wish to God I could do more.

STELLA: Goodbye and thank you *(she leaves)*.

FR. BARRY *picks up the phone and dials for telegrams.*

FR. BARRY: This is 629–7634, I want to send a telegram to Ireland to a Mr. Sean Healy – H-E-A-L-Y in Ahaderg, Co. Mayo. The message is, 'Deeply regret tell you all Mike died peacefully today. Please phone Father Barry –'

## Scene Eight

*Following morning. Interior* STELLA'S *flat. Christmas decorations up.* STELLA *and* MARLENE *sit over a cup of tea.* MARLENE *tries to cheer her up.* MARLENE *succeeds in her efforts when she's doing practical things, but her words of philosophy are falling on stony ground.*

MARLENE: I was just saying to Mrs. Hardy you know the one wot had the accident, I was just saying to her, well it's very hard on Stella, very hard and nobody can say otherwise but at least she has it over her, somehow there should be comfort in that. The rest of us have it ahead of us.

STELLA: Yes.

MARLENE: The way I live Stella, and I don't mind telling you this, the way I've kept my head above water over the last years is by seeking something cheerful everywhere. Now I mean everywhere. No matter how sad something is, I say 'What good can you see in that Marlene?' and I always find some good.

STELLA: It may work for you but I don't see any good I'm afraid. I just try to be a bit cheerful in front of the girls. Are they all right do you think?

MARLENE: They're fine love, they're sitting in front of the television and my two have instructions to give them more lemonade every time they see their glasses empty.

STELLA: I don't think they've ever seen television in the morning, that'll be a treat for them. They're very good really. Sharon cried a lot during the night.

MARLENE: Well she would wouldn't she, she's old enough to know what's happened, she'll miss her Dad. But the others bless them they're too young.

STELLA: *(thoughtfully)* I was the same age as Maureen when my father died, six, and yet I remember him very well.

MARLENE: Yes, well you would, but you'd remember more what people said about him afterwards. I bet your Mam would say things about your Dad for years afterwards and you thought that you remembered them yourself.

STELLA: My Mam hadn't a good word to say for my Dad.

MARLENE: Never mind love, it wasn't like that in this house.

STELLA: No, Mike was very good to me, and the quietest man you could meet. I can't believe he'll not be back saying 'Would yis stop all this caterwauling and get me a cup of tea?'

MARLENE: He was a very good husband to you, never forget that.

STELLA: when I think of some of the husbands ... not a few yards away for this door *(she lowers her voice as if a neighbour might overhear)*.

MARLENE: Well this is it isn't it? I'm amazed she hasn't gone funny in the head from the way he pushes her about.

STELLA: Mike never lifted a hand in his whole life.

MARLENE: He had respect for you, and he gave you all his wages to keep the place nice.

STELLA: He only kept a couple of quid for a few pints and a few cigarettes for himself ... and what he sent his mother in Ireland. All the rest was down on this table on Friday evening.

MARLENE: You'll always have a very happy memory of him, I've always said that.

STELLA: *(mistily)* He wouldn't work on the lump, he'd have earned more, but he said he'd be worried in case of an accident and nothing coming in for me and the children ... *(crying now)* He was so thoughtful Marlene, he thought of everything *(she breaks down totally)*.

MARLENE: Oh God, I know, I know. What we need is a glass of sherry. No, don't say you don't, I'll get it. Tom got some in for Christmas.

STELLA: *(mumbling and crying)* I don't w-a-n-t any sherry.

MARLENE *runs out to her own flat across the corridor, we hear her calling to* STELLA'S *children.*

MARLENE: Yes you do. I won't be a minute. Sharon if you want more lemonade or biscuits you just pour the glasses out ... *(back in* STELLA'S) Here we are – just a small glass, for the two of us. People always have a little sherry if they feel low.

STELLA: You're very kind. *(she blows her nose hard)* I'll have to stop this bawling.

MARLENE: I think you're being marvellous, I really do. Cheers.

STELLA: *(She looks around the room which is of course decorated with the tinsel and the paper streamers they bought and put up yesterday)* Those Christmas decorations will have to come down for a start. They're far too cheerful.

MARLENE: *(looking at them doubtfully)* Yes they are a bit bright. Here have another drop. Cheer you up.

## Scene Nine

*Stairs exterior centre* FR. BARRY *comes up the stairs and into the office.*

## Scene Ten

*Interior social centre.*

FR. BARRY: No word from those Healy's yet?

JACKY: Nothing while I was here.

FR. BARRY: You'd think we'd have heard from them by now. Aw, dear God, the problems of bloody communications in what's meant to be an age of mass communication.

JACKY: *(looking at a bit of paper)* Some fellow rang up earlier on wanting to know our address, that wouldn't have been them by any chance?

FR. BARRY: I don't know, why would it have been?

JACKY: Well – he sounded a bit confused. He thought this was a presbytery. I told him it was a centre, he didn't seem to take it in, he said he wanted Father Barry, so I told him you'd be in at eleven.

FR. BARRY: It could be one of Mike Healy's relatives, but what would they be messing around like that for? Aw, it could have been anyone.

## Scene Eleven

STELLA'S *flat*. STELLA *and* MARLENE *taking down the Christmas decorations.*

MARLENE: Will Father Barry be doing the service and everything for Mike?

STELLA: No, that will be in the parish church, but he's arranging everything. He said he'd come around and tell me when he heard from the family in Ireland. The Healy's weren't much at writing but I expect they'll telephone.

MARLENE: Well they will of course won't they? He was their brother. I don't suppose his mother will come over for the funeral?

STELLA: I hope to God she doesn't, she's over eighty.

MARLENE: Perhaps they might want a wake. You know like in the pictures with people singing and playing music and telling stories.

STELLA: *(outraged)* A wake, a drunken Irish wake here! They'd never want that. Not with the quiet way Mike lived. He wasn't the kind of man who'd have a wake.

MARLENE: Well they might want a bit of drink in the house you know Stella. I should mind my own business, but when Mrs. O'Brien's father, you know the old man who used to walk on two sticks until they gave him that thing like a supermarket trolley to walk with … anyway when he died, they had about twenty people in the house, and they had five crates of beer, I know because I was in the shop when poor Mrs. O'Brien came in to get it.

STELLA: Maybe you're right. I'd better get some sort of a drink in, they'll have come a long way. But I don't know how much to get and what. I don't even know how many of them are coming.

MARLENE: *(soothingly)* Look, don't worry, I shouldn't have brought it up at all. Listen, why don't you ask Father Barry about it. He'd know. It's his phone number on the telegram, right?

STELLA: Yes, of course. *(calmer now)* Yes, Father Barry's the man, he'd be able to tell me what to do.

## Scene Twelve

*Staircase outside the office. Two men are seen coming hesitantly up towards the office.*

## Scene Thirteen

*Interior centre. Day. Morning. They open the door. They look left and right taking in the place in what might be cunning or could be mere unease. FR. BARRY and JACKY look at them with some concern.*

SEAN HEALY: Good morning, is one of you able to tell me where I'd find Father Barry please.

FR. BARRY: Yes, I'm Jim Barry, what can I do for you.

SEAN: I'm Sean Healy and this is my brother Liam Healy. We are brothers of the late Michael Healy. We got your telegram and we came straight over.

FR. BARRY: *(somehow relieved that they have identified themselves)* Aw grand, grand, you got the telegram. Come in. Sit down, sit down. Um ... this is Jack West ... who's training to be a social worker.

JACKY: *(getting up)* I'm very pleased ...

SEAN: *(looking around)* Is this a class of an addition to the church?

FR. BARRY: No, no nothing like that. It's a voluntary citizens help centre, we do every kind of thing here, mainly helping people to cope with ... well you won't want to be hearing all of that. Sit down, sit down. We're very sorry about your brother, Sean, he was a great fellow.

SEAN: *(a little surprised to be addressed by his first name)* Uh … yes, uh, Father he was of course. Are you an order man Father or a priest of the parish?

FR. BARRY: *(who is in a polo-necked sweater)* Is it the gear? Yerra no priest who's working in welfare puts on proper garb nowadays unless they're visiting. Have you been to see Stella and the children or did you come straight here?

SEAN: Oh we came here straight Father.

LIAM: Without pausing on the way.

FR. BARRY: *(a bit at a loss)* Well, yes, fine. Now what would you say to a cup of tea, I'm sure Jacky could …

JACKY: Yes that would be no trouble.

SEAN: No thank you Father. I suppose we'd better get things organised.

LIAM: Yes, that would be the best.

FR. BARRY: Right. Your brother's body is still in the hospital morgue. Tonight it's moved to a funeral home, tomorrow evening we'll go to the Church and you can have the funeral mass the next morning. Father Flanagan is going to say the Mass, he's a good friend of Stella and Mike's. He runs the children's club that young Sharon is in. Will there be any more of the family coming over do you think?

SEAN: No, there won't.

LIAM: It's just us.

*An awkward silence.* FR. BARRY *half looks at* JACKY *who goes and busies himself with files down at the other end of the room.*

FR. BARRY: Tell me is anything wrong? I mean is there anything you're trying to tell me. I get this feeling that something's not being said.

SEAN: Well I didn't know it was going to be like this at all.

LIAM: In a small office with a plain-clothes priest.

SEAN: I thought it was going to be more ... you know authorities and telling the priest and straightening it all out.

LIAM: And being done with it.

SEAN: And bringing him home.

FR. BARRY: Bringing him home where?

SEAN: Back home with us to the churchyard in Ahaderg.

FR. BARRY: *(his face clearing a bit but still seeing storms ahead)* Oh, I see you'd like him buried in Ireland. Is that it?

LIAM: Yes that's it really.

SEAN: It's for the best that he's buried there, that's why we're here – to bring him home.

FR. BARRY: Well if you'll explain ...

LIAM: It's what's expected.

FR. BARRY: *(trying to be sympathetic)* You mean his mother wants it done that way, is that it? *(pause)* Is that the heart of it?

SEAN: His wife wants it done that way.

FR. BARRY: But Stella didn't say to me ...

SEAN: His wife and his children want his body to
come home. They want to walk behind it up the
hill on Sunday afternoon. That's why we're here.

*There is a silence in which the noises of the room seem loud.
The traffic from the street, distant carols, peoples' voices
outside in a corridor perhaps.* FR. BARRY *gets up and goes to
the window.*

FR. BARRY: He had a wife and children in Ireland?

SEAN: Oh yes, yes.

FR. BARRY: But he couldn't have.

LIAM: Oh but Father, he's been married to Maureen
for over twenty years

SEAN: For a good three years before he ever came
to England.

FR. BARRY: Aw no, God no. Not Stella and Mike
Healy.

SEAN: Sure he had to go to England to get work.

LIAM: There was nothing for him.

SEAN: He had to go.

FR. BARRY: How many children did you say?

SEAN: Nine, five boys and four girls.

FR. BARRY: *(whirling around)* NINE.

SEAN: Oh they're fine, they do very well, the days
of the tail end of family getting nothing are over.

They're off on buses to school and the young ones would buy and sell you, they're so bright.

FR. BARRY: ... I don't believe a word of this, he can't have young children over in the West of Ireland. In the name of God. Mike Healy! A working man can't have a family of nine children, it's ridiculous.

LIAM: Oh the family's there Father, there's no denying it.

FR. BARRY: What about Stella, she doesn't know any of this. What about Stella and the three little girls down the road here?

SEAN: Oh we don't know anything about that I'm afraid.

LIAM: No, we don't know any Stella, we just came to take Mike's body back home where it belongs and to have him buried where his wife and children can go and pray for him at his grave.

FR. BARRY: (*very cross*) Come on out of that, you know very well about Stella. Who did you think sent you the telegram?

SEAN: Well it was your phone number that was given on it Father.

LIAM: It said 'Contact Father Barry'.

FR. BARRY: (*calmer*) Well did you know, or do you know now that he has a wife and three children in this country. That makes two wives and a dozen children. Beautiful. I'm telling you now, he has a very nice wife, a grand woman who lives with her three little daughters. And she and I have arranged Mike Healy's funeral *(his voice raises)* and it's all to be taking place here, just outside this door and across by the traffic lights, the church is up there.

SEAN: *(calmly)* But we have to bring him home Father.

FR. BARRY: But this *is* his home, this is where he lived for fifty weeks out of the year for nearly twenty years. In the name of God, isn't this his home!

SEAN: But he has a wife and children in Ireland, Father. Maureen's his wife in the eyes of God and the Church and the law of course.

LIAM: It's not as if he ever left Maureen.

FR. BARRY: I never heard of such hypocrisy, you must have known he had left Maureen, you must have known he'd got married again.

SEAN: Sure he couldn't have got married again.

LIAM: Not if he was married already.

FR. BARRY: But he hardly ever saw the poor woman in Ireland, he wasn't her husband at all.

SEAN: He supported her, every week he sent her what he could.

FR. BARRY: Don't be telling me lies, he couldn't have supported her, he was an ordinary working man who supported his wife and family here. How could he have supported a whole brood in Ireland?

SEAN: *(levelly)* He sent her a ten pound note up to two Fridays ago, every single Friday. It came on Monday in a registered envelope.

LIAM: Over all the years.

SEAN: And he came home every August for a fortnight.

FR. BARRY: Did he?

SEAN: Well, wouldn't any man who works hard all year want to come home to his own family for the holidays?

SEAN: *(he opens a wallet)* I have the address of this undertaker here Father, he arranges funerals to Ireland. He organises all the details like getting permission to put a coffin on the plane or the boat.

LIAM: So we thought that you might get in touch with him for us ... and ...

FR. BARRY *comes back from the window and pounds on the desk by which the two brothers are sitting.*

FR. BARRY: I'll get in touch with nobody. Christ! I'm very sorry for the pair of you. Don't think I'm not. But please, please could you stop talking as if Stella and the children didn't exist.

SEAN: But don't you see Father that if there is this woman and ... and everything, that it really can be no business of ours. Maureen will be expecting us to do what we said we'd do. Not sitting down and talking about the rights and wrongs of the world.

FR. BARRY: But doesn't Maureen have some idea that he has a wife, he had a wife over here? She must know.

LIAM: I don't know what she thinks to herself, but she never said anything. That's for certain.

SEAN: And it's not a wife, Father, you don't seem to understand that at all. This ... er woman ... couldn't be Mike's wife. They weren't married you know.

FR. BARRY: They were married in that Church over there about thirteen years ago. That's where Michael and Stella were married I tell you.

SEAN: *(genuinely amazed)* But how could he have got letters of freedom?

FR. BARRY: Oh ... to hell with letters of freedom. Anyone can write a letter of shaggin' freedom. Isn't it true? All you have to be able to do is to be able to write and head the paper the 'Presbytery Ahaderg go wherever you want to'. Priests here aren't trained in the Special Branch, they don't say 'Aha, Aha, this could be a phoney letter of freedom, let's put a team on to it'. They think people are normal.

*He looks at the two brothers sitting like tweedledum and tweedledee.*

FR. BARRY: Who's going to tell Stella. Oh my God. Who's going to tell her? *(there is no answer from the brothers, almost to himself)* If you pair go down to the flat God know what might happen. I go down by myself and tell her it's very humiliating for her. I don't know what to do. Right, we'll all go together, then I can ... I don't know what I can do, play with the children or something. C'mon, we'll go now.

SEAN: Without meaning to be disrespectful Father I don't think ...

FR. BARRY: Let me put it to you this way, if you want one more word of this discussed it's discussed in Stella Healy's flat. Do you get me?

SEAN: But we have the law on our side, I mean she's not his legal wife, it's a bigamous marriage if it took place at all.

LIAM: The law would say we have a right to his body.

FR. BARRY: The law here has little time for antics like this.

SEAN: I don't know ...

FR. BARRY: For God's sake you're not committing yourself to anything beyond the common decency of coming with me to this woman's flat. *(to JACKY)* I'm sorry about all this Jacky you know ... just keep things ticking over. Hold off what you can.

JACKY: *(who has been listening to every word of the exchange)* Fine Father.

FR. BARRY: Come on fellows will you come on till we face this bloody thing.

*They leave the centre.*

## PART TWO

## Scene Fourteen

*Staircase outside* STELLA's *flat.*

FR. BARRY *and two brothers come to the door of* STELLA'S *flat. They stand awkwardly waiting for the door to be answered.* STELLA *is a long time answering the door, there is no conversation, but the brothers look around a bit taking in their surroundings. Finally the door is answered.*

STELLA: Oh ... Father, I'm sorry to have kept you waiting.

FR. BARRY: Stella, these are Mike's brothers, Sean and Liam.

STELLA: Oh I see.

FR. BARRY: Can we come in do you think?

STELLA: *(embarrassed)* Oh yes, of course.

*They go in and stand awkwardly around.*

FR. BARRY: They came to me first.

STELLA: *(gauchely)* Well I'm very glad you're here. There was no need of coming over in one way, but in another of course, he was your brother and I think it was very ...

FR. BARRY: Can we sit down?

STELLA: Yes, what am I thinking about, I'm still only half realising things I think. Um, I'm afraid

I'm not sure which ... *(she looks helplessly from one to another and back at* FR. BARRY *a bit surprised that the priest hasn't been helping her out).*

*Small and very awkward silence.* FR. BARRY *determined not to help out stares directly ahead of him. Finally,*

STELLA: Well could I offer you a cup of tea. I don't have any drink in the house but I'll get some if you are thinking of having ... well a few drinks. I don't expect it will be a wake, but you know a few drinks.

LIAM: Look Mrs. would you sit down, my brother here and the priest, they have a few things to say, like, a few questions to ask.

STELLA: *(upset)* Well he died of pneumonia, virus pneumonia, the ones you can't cure with ordinary drugs, and I don't know why he got it I'm sure. And *(begins to cry)* I don't know why he had to die so unexpected like at Christmas. And I don't know why you are all sitting looking at me as if ... as if ... as if I had two heads or something?

FR. BARRY: Well go on Liam, Sean, go on. You said it was very straightforward, let's hear it.

SEAN: There's a complication about the late Michael Healy. I don't find this easy, but since I'm the one that has to say it ... *(he looks balefully at the priest and his brother)* this is it. Michael Healy had a marriage going in Ireland before he ever met you Mam, and so the contract he went through with you was no real contract. Not a real marriage.

STELLA: Is that a joke or what?

SEAN: No you asked to be told the truth and that's it. As I said, I'm very sorry but you asked me to tell you.

STELLA: *(stunned)* I didn't ask you to tell me anything.

LIAM: *(embarrassed for her and sympathetic – but still a coward)* Go on Sean, tell her that nobody blames her, it must have been some real mix up.

SEAN: I'm telling it straight out which nobody else has the guts to do.

STELLA: Is this some awful thing Father or is it only a joke? Please Father why aren't you saying anything. Tell me.

FR. BARRY: Stella, they're saying that Mike had a wife and kids in Ireland all the time he was married to you.

STELLA: Not seriously Father, they don't mean it seriously ...

FR. BARRY: They do. All right lads, I just wanted you to say it straight out more to convince myself that you meant it. Stella, he was married to this woman, but it wasn't a real relationship, you know that. Didn't he live with you, here, in this flat, now stay still, sit where you are.

STELLA: It can't be true. I don't believe it. I won't believe it.

FR. BARRY: *(trying to hold her hand)* Listen, listen, he and you got married, you had three lovely girls, you had thirteen or fourteen good years together. That's what was real, that's what Mike Healy had for a life, not something he was doing out of duty. Not a bit of paper and a couple of quid posted in a registered envelope on Fridays.

STELLA: That was for his mother.

FR. BARRY: No. They say it was for his wife, Stella. This is the hard bit. What you have to do is to accept that she exists, and also at the same time accept that it can't change, it doesn't ever change all the good things there were between you and Mike. Do you understand me?

STELLA: You're saying he was married before he met me?

FR. BARRY: A different life, different times.

STELLA: So our wedding day wasn't his first wedding at all, he'd been through it all already.

FR. BARRY: But it's totally different.

STELLA: He must have married her when he was very young.

SEAN: *(because she addressed the remark to him)* I suppose he was, what age was he Liam? Twenty four, twenty six? Maureen would have been a couple of years younger. Say twenty six Mam.

STELLA: Maureen.

FR. BARRY: You do realise that she's still alive, that's what the whole excitement is about. She's a young woman like yourself, with a big family over in Ireland and they want ...

STELLA: I suppose all her children are grown up now *(everyone exchanges glances)* ... well they are aren't they?

LIAM: *(bluntly not realising the implication immediately)* Well the youngest lad's only around four.

STELLA: *(looking at him unbelievingly)* Four? Four years of age, what are you talking about. Sure Mike and I have been married for thirteen years. You can't come into my house and say he has a four year old child by some other woman. Father you're not going to let him say that.

LIAM: It's not some other woman. You're the one who's the other woman. Maureen's the mother of his nine children, and we're bringing Mike's body back to her. That's why we're here.

STELLA: *(half standing up, half laughing, looking from SEAN to LIAM)* Nine children, take his body to Ireland, don't be ridiculous. You must be mad, it must be another Mike Healy you know. *(triumphantly)* That's it Father. There was some mistake, the telegram was sent to the wrong family *(she laughs a bit hysterically at this)*.

LIAM: *(pointing at a picture of MIKE and STELLA on their wedding day)* That's our brother Mike in the photo there Mam.

STELLA: *(now utterly broken)* It's not possible, he couldn't have had nine children over there. It's not possible *(she puts her head down on the table)*. Lies, lies, year after year. 'Don't come home to Ireland with me, it's too dear, the old woman is getting a bit old anyway'. I believed him – everyone believed him. But 'twas all lies. T'wasn't only his mother he used to be going home to see. Is there any mother at all?

SEAN: Oh yes, our mother is alive and well, God keep her so. She's over eighty now, but in great form.

STELLA: And where do Maureen and all these children live?

SEAN: They live with our mother. And with Martin, he's the eldest of the family, he lives in the house.

STELLA: And is your mother, is she fond of this Maureen ... I mean does she get on well with her?

LIAM: Sure anyone would get on with Maureen, she's a grand woman.

SEAN: *(a bit more tactfully)* Well seeing how they've lived together for so long and shared the bringing up of the children in a way, they have a lot in common you know Liam.

LIAM: And the hens and the place and all.

STELLA: And what's she like – this Maureen?

LIAM: *(tactlessly but loyally)* Well she's a fine woman, a fair haired girl with a great heart and a great smile for everyone. And of course she's had a very hard life.

SEAN: *(gently)* A lot of people have had hard lives Liam.

*Silence.*

STELLA: *(much more calmly)* Are you sure about all this. I mean it's all really true?

FR. BARRY: I'm afraid it is.

STELLA: So what happens now Father. I mean it's a competition isn't it? There's that woman over there who's had the hard life and me here who's had it nice and easy. She had to look after nine children – I only had three. She had to cook for a brother-in-law and a mother-in-law when I was out playing bingo. She only got £8–£10 a week while I got nearly £40. She only had him for a few weeks a year while I had him for years on end. And we each want to be considered his wife. It's like something out of the Old Testament.

FR. BARRY: If it is I can't remember what they did about it.

SEAN: It's more a matter of what's right Mam. That's why we're here. I admit I didn't want to come and talk to you.

STELLA: I wish you'd never come.

LIAM: But we had to come … for his body, you know.

STELLA: *(almost in a scream)* What do you mean for his body.

SEAN: The remains. The coffin. We have to take it home.

STELLA: Well that's one thing you're not going to do. Mike Healy had his own reasons for all the lies he told, but he's going to rest here in his own parish. Isn't he Father, he can't be taken away?

SEAN: But that's why we came.

FR. BARRY: Stella, I had to bring them here. They thought it was a matter of cancelling a funeral here and having one there. They didn't know anything of your life, that's why I brought them here to you.

STELLA: *(very calm now)* Well, I don't want them here any more Father. Please go, everyone.

LIAM: But is it understood that ...

SEAN: Shut up Liam.

LIAM: But the whole point of ...

SEAN: Did you hear me?

STELLA: Please Father, I'd like to be by myself.

FR. BARRY: Sure Stella, sure.

STELLA: *(keeping calm as if with difficulty)* So if you could all go now please.

FR. BARRY: Come on. *(more or less nudging the others into a standing position)* There's a pub down on the corner, we'll go and have a pint there and talk on a bit. Stella can I come back and talk to you later on?

STELLA: Yes, I'll be here.

SEAN: At least you have ...

STELLA: Yes?

SEAN: Oh nothing. I wasn't saying anything.

STELLA: What did she do, Maureen. When she heard Mike was dead.

SEAN: Oh she went and told the priest.

STELLA: *(looking cynically at* FR. BARRY) So did I. Isn't that funny?

*The men leave clumping down the stairs.* STELLA *remains alone in the room.*

## Scene Fifteen

*Interior of an Irish pub in Kilburn, which would in fact be like an Irish pub anywhere except Ireland. There would be pictures of hurling teams and Irish dolls and souvenirs made in Galway among the bottles. An Irish calendar on the wall. Irish dance music on the juke box.*

FR. BARRY: Over here fellows *(finding a place for them)* What will you have?

SEAN: I'll get them.

FR. BARRY: No, will you let me get a drink. What'll it be?

SEAN: The young fella'll come over and take our order.

FR. BARRY: *(wearily)* They don't do that in London, that's only an Irish thing.

LIAM: But this is a lounge bar.

FR. BARRY: It is and it isn't, it's a saloon. I'm having a pint of bitter.

SEAN: I'll have Guinness.

LIAM: A pint of stout.

FR. BARRY: It mightn't be the same as back home – the way they pour it.

LIAM: Sure nothing's the same as back home.

FR. BARRY *goes up to the counter to get the drinks.* SEAN *and* LIAM *settle themselves uneasily into their corner looking about them.*

LIAM: It's not like being in England at all, it's just like home in a way.

SEAN: They say there are more Irish here than in Dublin.

LIAM: I thought that was meant to be Liverpool.

SEAN: Or was it Boston. Sure it doesn't matter anyway.

LIAM: What do you think of your man?

SEAN: He seems decent enough, he's one of these order priests you know. They do ordinary jobs in the day and they live in a monastery at night.

LIAM: How do you know that?

SEAN: Well, what else would he be doing, running that workers' place? That couldn't be his only life as a priest. I mean he might as well just be any kind of local official if he didn't live in a monastery.

LIAM: Yeah, I suppose so. Do you think it'll be difficult with yer woman.

SEAN: The priest should really have gone himself and told her, you know. I'd say she was a fine looking woman when she was younger.

LIAM: Did you see the holy pictures on the wall, could you beat that?

SEAN: (crossly) Sometimes you're as thick as the wall. That woman got herself married in a church, she went to mass and communion and all, she thought she was properly married, there's no reason for her not to have holy pictures.

(FR. BARRY *returns*)

LIAM: Oh, thank you Father, thanks. Good luck to you.

FR. BARRY: Slainte.

SEAN: Good Luck.

LIAM: Do you go home yourself to Ireland much Father?

FR. BARRY: I used to, not much now though. Now – now you've met her, and all, do you still want to take his body back to Ireland?

SEAN: But Father, that has nothing to do with her being a nice decent woman. Surely you know that. It's just what has to be done.

LIAM: That's what we came to do.

FR. BARRY: I know it's what you *came* to do but I don't see why it has to be done. The man is out of his home town for near to twenty years. His life was lived over here.

SEAN: That's not the point.

FR. BARRY: Well it is the point in a way. He's not known there, he's not missed day by day like he will be here. It's only in the summer people will remember he didn't come home for his annual holiday.

LIAM: But everyone knows he died. It's known.

FR. BARRY: Look, why don't you just go to the funeral here and say when you got back that it was thought better that he be buried where he had lived.

SEAN: I don't think you understand at all Father. Nobody at home thinks Mike lived in Kilburn. They think he worked in Kilburn, but he lived back home. That's where his place is, and his family.

FR. BARRY: *(amazed)* Would they think that about all emigrants?

SEAN: It would depend.

LIAM: On whether they came back regularly.

SEAN: And looked after their family.

FR. BARRY: *(depressed)* Oh God.

LIAM: It has to be where he's buried.

SEAN: You see his life would have no meaning if he were left here. What would be the whole point of going to England and working like a dog for a living if he wasn't brought home to lie in peace when he died.

FR. BARRY: *(stunned)* I see.

SEAN: Do you Father, that's a relief. I was afraid you didn't see what we were on about.

FR. BARRY: And I was afraid you didn't see what Stella was on about.

SEAN: I don't think there's a bit of blame attached to that woman.

LIAM: No, she never knew that she did any wrong.

FR. BARRY: She didn't do any wrong. She did nothing but right and look at where it got her.

SEAN: And Maureen didn't do any wrong either Father. She has no idea of all this.

LIAM: Be fair, she may have had a suspicion.

SEAN: We've no way of knowing, she's said nothing. And I'm going to say nothing, I hope you're going to do the same.

LIAM: I'll keep my own counsel. Father can I get you another. The same is it?

FR. BARRY: *(standing up, looking very weary)* No, no if you'll excuse me. I want to go back to the office for a bit – then I may go back to Stella ... look you'll be here for a half an hour anyway. You could have your lunch here, they serve food too.

SEAN: All right Father we'll wait for you.

LIAM: Will you be long then Father?

SEAN: He'll be as long as it takes that's all.

FR. BARRY: *(dazed)* Yes as long as it takes.

## Scene Sixteen

*Interior* FR. BARRY'S *office.*

JACKY *is in the middle of a conversation with a truculent and aggressive looking woman. She is holding a baby in her arms.*

WOMAN: ... what can the police do, they're not our friends, the police don't care if I live or die, they're not coming in there to rescue me. So who's going to look after me if he comes in again drunk to beat me up.

JACKY: Look Mrs. Wylie, I've made arrangements for you to go to the women's shelter.

WOMAN: The shelter. If I go to the bleeding shelter, he'll take over my place, do I have to stay in the shelter for the rest of my life. Father Barry knew how to put the frighteners on him (FR. BARRY *enters*) ... Oh there you are Father, Ted's back again.

FR. BARRY: Not now love.

WOMAN: He's back you don't understand ... he came in last night and ...

FR. BARRY: Not NOW, Jacky get her into the shelter.

JACKY: She doesn't want to go.

FR. BARRY: She doesn't want her head opened either. Get yourself and the kids into that shelter in the next hour. No, I won't hear another word, go on home – that's the best I can do.

*Woman, dazed and disappointed, leaves – the violence of his attitude brooks no argument.*

JACKY: *(also shocked)* What happened? How did it go?

FR. BARRY: I'm not giving him up just because of what some one horse town in the West of Ireland are going to say. I'm not doing it. Do you know, that people in Ahaderg, whatever it is think, that Mike Healy doesn't live in Kilburn, that he lives back there with them, he only works here! Only *works* here mind you, like some kind of super commuter, I suppose.

JACKY: Well, if they believe that, they'll believe anything.

FR. BARRY: Maybe it makes the whole thing more bearable, if they can see fellows heading off for London forever and pretend they've gone to do a day's work ...

JACKY: Well, I presume you've told them you're not going to help them?

FR. BARRY: I've told them nothing, I've left them sitting in Fred's bar down there looking at each other. You see, on other hand, she's had nothing either. Nothing at all.

JACKY: Who?

FR. BARRY: Maureen.

JACKY: Who's she?

FR. BARRY: *(impatiently)* The Irish wife, the first wife, the real wife.

JACKY: But you were saying earlier that Stella was his wife, that she has rights.

FR. BARRY: *(in a roar of pain)* Christ – don't you think I KNOW! Why should Stella give up her husband for a whole lot of meaningless rituals she doesn't even understand? If the Catholic Church in this country thought Mike was good enough to marry her in a Catholic Church then they can think he's good enough to be buried here, not packed up on a neat undertaker's charter flight.

JACKY: They can't insist you know. Two families fighting over the one body. I don't think the authorities here would let them take the body out of the country. There'd be the most god awful fuss.

FR. BARRY: But they're right to want him home aren't they? I mean look at it from their point of view. It would be a very odd life if after all these years of his coming home on holiday and sending the few quid on a Friday they decided he might as well be buried in England. You see that's *their* way of looking at it. There's a bit of dignity in a tombstone Jacky, and they might make such a fuss of them over in Ireland. Yes, maybe a tombstone isn't much to give Maureen after all the years.

JACKY: As a kind of a consolation prize.

FR. BARRY: *(cross now)* Yes as a consolation prize. We have damn all else to give, certainly no solutions.

JACKY: *(taken aback)* Nobody is asking you for a solution, you're not the Home Office. You don't have to do anything.

FR. BARRY: Don't I?

JACKY: You don't have to play God.

FR. BARRY: If I don't would you tell me why are there two men in shiny suits down in Fred's waiting for me to say yes or no? And what is a woman doing up in the Council flats waiting for me to say yes or no. If that isn't being asked for a solution I don't know what is. *(pause)*

JACKY: *(subdued)* If you knew Mike Healy here, then here is where you should let him stay.

FR. BARRY: That's what I feel. But I don't feel it *certainly* enough to be able to fight for it.

JACKY: You've always told me here that you'd go mad if you argued every case out in terms of who was most deserving. Are the Cypriots who have no English worse off than the Bengalis who have no relations? Which family should we put in the house? You said that you kind of know these things, that you feel them, and you do them, and you don't sit around crying in case you've made the wrong choice, you're on making the next one. I found that very helpful, can't you do it here?

FR. BARRY: It's too pat.

JACKY: *(hurt)* Well they're your words.

FR. BARRY: It's still too pat. Too glib.

JACKY: Oh Mike Healy, you bastard, look at all the hurt you're causing.

FR. BARRY: Maybe he was far far less of a bastard than anyone else. Is it all that bad wanting a decent home and a family?

JACKY: But you can't keep starting decent homes and families all over the place.

FR. BARRY: Would he have been better pissed on a Saturday night trying to find a woman, and hating himself for it and hating her? Would that have made his years here more valuable? Is that what we admire in a good decent Irishman?

JACKY: It's not a choice between one or the other.

FR. BARRY: What would you know about it, you don't know the Irish, you were born here, you didn't have to leave! What do I know about it? I left Ireland from choice because this is where I wanted to work – it still is. *(pause)* You see, you can look at it in terms of places or in terms of numbers.

JACKY: I don't know what you mean.

FR. BARRY: Places. There or here. I don't know them there, I know them here, I know that here is good and simple and trusting. I only have the two beauties words that there is good.

JACKY: Well yes.

FR. BARRY: Or just numbers, pure simple numbers. One woman here, lousy hard life, shift work in a factory, suddenly told her that the husband is not her husband. Should some churchman, me to pick one at random, not say to her, forget all that rubbish, I'll get him buried here as your husband, that's what he believed he was and we believed he was.

JACKY: *(hopefully)* Well isn't that what you're going to do?

FR. BARRY: One woman there, lousy hard life, living up a little borreen in Connaught, the mad old granny, the mad old uncles, one wife and three children, one wife and nine children.

JACKY: But ...

FR. BARRY: Three children, nine children. Three children plus a few neighbours, nine children plus a whole village.

## Scene Seventeen

STELLA'S *flat later that day.* STELLA is *sitting silently. The TV is on with the sound off.* FR. BARRY *comes in. Very long silence. He pulls up a chair. But says nothing.*

STELLA: *(ice-cold)* They can have him. They can take him off to Ireland. I don't want him. Go back to the pub and tell them.

FR. BARRY: You can't go and say something like that.

STELLA: I've said it. Why don't you go back and tell them. They might even sing a song. The Irish are so good at singing. It's what you wanted me to do isn't it. Be honest. I'd like someone to be honest for once. Isn't that what you were going to ask me to do? Isn't that what you were going to say?

FR. BARRY: In a way yes.

STELLA: In what way? It was what you were going to ask me to do.

FR. BARRY: I have no power, Stella, to ask you to do anything at all. I'm the priest who runs the centre, I'm nothing to do with you except a friend.

STELLA: A friend.

FR. BARRY: I don't decide. I don't decide any more than Marlene decides, than Jimmy down in the paper shop decides. People ask my advice about things simply because I meet a lot of people through my work. Not because I'm any law, that's why I'm trying hard to think what's best.

STELLA: And you have haven't you?

FR. BARRY: If you ask me, then I do say that I think it's probably a kind thing to let them take his body back to Ireland.

STELLA: *(sighing almost in satisfaction at being proved right)* Oh yes.

FR. BARRY: It's not as if you need tombstones and monuments and people parading through a street. You've had your life with him, they've had nothing, that's why.

STELLA: And also because it would cause less talk.

FR. BARRY: What do you mean?

STELLA: No gossip about fancy women and bastards.

FR. BARRY: Don't use words like that about yourself and your children.

STELLA: It's what we are.

FR. BARRY: It's not what you are in anyone's eyes.

STELLA: In the law? Do I have a right to anything he owned? No! In the church, do they think now that my union with him was blessed? No! In the eyes of society am I married? If he has a wife and family in Ireland who take his body back and bury it and pat the ground over it, then people here can't think I'm married to Mike.

STELLA: I'll sign whatever they want to take the body of their brother home to his wife, for all the dancing and the singing and the wakes. And the wasn't-he-the-fine-fellow bit. You can go down to the pub and have another nice Christmas drink with them and tell them that.

FR. BARRY: Perhaps if I leave you to yourself you won't feel you hate everyone so much.

STELLA: Perhaps.

FR. BARRY: But I have a feeling that this is the time you need me – somebody, Father Flanagan?

STELLA: Not Father Flanagan thank you, not Father anything.

FR. BARRY: Stella what can I do to tell you that there's some kind of friendship, some help however watery it may seem ...

STELLA: Forget it Father, that's the best.

FR. BARRY: Stella.

STELLA: Please don't keep me calling me Stella.

FR. BARRY: Well, I can't keep calling you Mrs. Healy.

STELLA: That's just it. I'm not Mrs Healy am I? I never was.

*They look at each other for a long time.*

## Scene Eighteen

*The Centre.*

*A cold Sunday.* FR. BARRY *wears his priest's collar.*

JACKY *at the typewriter.*

JACKY: *(shrugging)* Listen, did I tell you the paper rang again, that guy who does the big feature pieces. He wants to do one about the Centre. What do you think? It'd be great publicity – in the New Year. God knows how much money we might get in.

FR. BARRY: Um.

JACKY: You know the kind of thing he does – 'The People who solve your Problems ... Any Problems we deal with it', what do you think of it?

FR. BARRY: *(walks to window in silence. Looking out at the rain)* I wasn't thinking of that, I was thinking they must be burying Mike Healy about now ... I was wondering about – about giving his life some meaning – that's what they said. That was what I was thinking.

THE END

It's well over a quarter of a century since I wrote this piece. It was based on a true story which I heard from a priest in London. I changed all the peoples' names and the place names and gave it in as my Christmas column for *The Irish Times*.

Several years later Louis Lentin who was then the Head of Drama in RTÉ suggested that I write it as a television play, he said it had relevance, and a beginning, middle and end. With his help and encouragement I wrote it and I will never forget the night I saw it going out on RTÉ. I thought it was TERRIFIC! I had totally forgotten that I supposedly had written it because it was just a story coming to life. There were great performances from Joan O'Hara and Donall Farmer, and from the late Pat Layde and Mona Baptiste.

I went to my own uncle's funeral the very next day and everyone there was talking about it.

And very soon the letters started coming in. Some of them were tearful, some were angry, some were outraged. They were from different parts of the country all of them saying the same thing. "How dare you tell our story?" Something that I didn't know in the 1970s, and indeed the priest who told me the story didn't know either, was that this pattern was being repeated all over the place. Men going to England to find work and forming another relationship, returning to Ireland once a year to see the original family. Yet as the priest in the play asks … was it such a terrible thing when you think about it? The alternatives were often depression, alcoholism and an aching loneliness and bitterness at being so far from home.

When we talk about the Good Old Days with pink tinted spectacles we might do well to remember a time over thirty years ago when our fellow Irish were forced to emigrate to earn a living. Somehow the old days look a lot less good and our own times much more healthy and hopeful in comparison.

When other drama groups perform this play, as I hope they will, it will be as an episode of history, and not something with which people all over the country can identify with any more.

Maeve Binchy
Dublin, 2005

In 1980 Arlen House commenced the re-publication of classic works by Irish women writers, which allowed a succession of forgotten and marginalised authors to enter the public and academic worlds in both Ireland and abroad. The result was, according to Anthony Roche, a key "development of Irish rather than London-based publishing, and a major step in the rewriting of the Irish literary canon" (*Ordinary People Dancing*, E. Walshe, Editor, Cork University Press).

This new series of Arlen Classic Literature hopes to emulate in some ways the ground-breaking work of Catherine Rose and Eavan Boland, amongst others. We start the series with the best known Irish woman writer – who also happens to be one of the world's favourite writers – but who has an often forgotten past (and present) as a writer of literary fiction.

Maeve Binchy started her literary career with a series of stage and television plays and brave and original short fiction, alongside her lauded journalistic work. Turning her hand to novels in the 1980s she gained enormous international commercial success, but was then marginalised as the queen of romantic fiction writing "chick-lit", to the disdain of literary critics and snobs, and sadly even by many feminists.

The re-publication of *Deeply Regretted By ...* will, I hope, contribute to the re-examination of Binchy's many books and demonstrate that her work clearly belongs to the Irish literary canon.

Alan Hayes
Publisher, Arlen House
Galway, 2005

# ARLEN CLASSIC LITERATURE

1      *Deeply Regretted By ...* / Maeve Binchy

2      *Lift Up Your Gates* / Maura Laverty

3      *The Female Line: Northern Irish Women Writers*
      Ruth Carr, Editor

4      *Grania* / Emily Lawless

## BACK LIST
*published between 1980–1987*

| | |
|---|---|
| Kate O'Brien: | *The Ante-Room* |
| | *The Last of Summer* |
| | *The Land of Spices* |
| Janet McNeill: | *The Maiden Dinosaur* |
| Anne Crone: | *Bridie Steen* |
| Norah Hoult: | *Holy Ireland* |
| Katharine Keane: | *Who Goes Home?* |
| | |
| Janet Madden-Simpson: Editor | *Woman's Part: An anthology of short fiction by and about Irish women 1890–1960* |